Princess Kamala

and

The Dogon Oracle

By

Barbara Solomon

Princess Kamala
and
The Dogon Oracle

By
Barbara Solomon

Printed in the United States of America.

ISBN-13: 978-1-54565-973-1

Dedication

I dedicate this book to Dr. Bernice Irene Evans. Dr. Evans holds three doctoral degrees, one in Economics, one in Education, and one honorary doctorate degree in Law. She is the matriarch of our family, an educator, a leader in her community, and a blessing to all who know her. Known as Aunt Bernice to family members, she is the only person I know who exemplifies the Princess Kamala character. I was fortunate to be a member of her family through marriage to her brother, Prince Evans, now deceased. Dr. Evans grew up with four siblings, two brothers and two sisters, all deceased. She has no children of her own, but has become a mother to all her siblings' children and grandchildren. They have always depended on her wisdom, advice, guidance, and love to grow and develop. Dr. Evans is more than an aunt; she is also a Queen Mother to her family, friends, and community. If she were living in twelfth-century ancient Africa, she would sit on the king's council of elders.

"She openeth her mouth with wisdom; and her tongue is the law of kindness. Give her of the fruit of her hands; and let her own works praise her in the gates."

Proverbs 31: 26, 31

Acknowledgement

Illustrator: Adamu Dauda:

Mr. Dauda was born in Accra, Ghana, and has resided there for the past thirty years. I found Mr. Dauda over a year ago on the Internet. He had posted some of his paintings on his Facebook page. I was awestruck by the vivid colors, design arrangement, and subject matter. I foresaw a marriage between his art and the story of my next book.

Mr. Dauda started painting at age of thirteen. He became motivated by visiting the cinemas and trying to draw the faces he saw on the movie posters. Mr. Dauda is a man of many talents. He teaches African dance to youth and is a very prolific painter, producing many paintings that can be viewed on his Facebook page. At present, Mr. Dauda is unmarried with no children, which allows him ample time to devote to his artwork. Mr. Dauda's work can be viewed on his Facebook page at: Adamu Dauda. You will not be disappointed.

Terms You Need to Know

Dogon Symbolism: This was created to preserve the Dogon religion. Without the symbols, the religion's meaning would have been lost over time. The religious beliefs are based on knowledge transferred from immortal beings, who travelled to earth from distant stars.

Nummo/Nommo: These were visitors from a distant planet who taught the Dogon about the stars, aspects of their religion, and knowledge of DNA.

Sirius: The Dogon believe that the brightest star in the night sky is Sirius. Based on Dogon mythology, Sirius is the center orbit for two tiny companion stars.

Hermaphrodite (Her-maph-ro-dite): A person or animal having both male and female sex organs, or other sexual characteristics or (in the case of some organisms) as the natural condition.

Poultice (poul-tice): A soft mass of typically plant material or flour, usually heated, and applied to the body to relieve soreness and inflammation, kept in place with a cloth.

Dogon Symbols

Sirius Orbit

Present Day West Africa

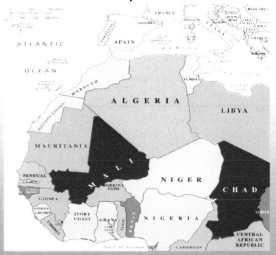

III

Introduction

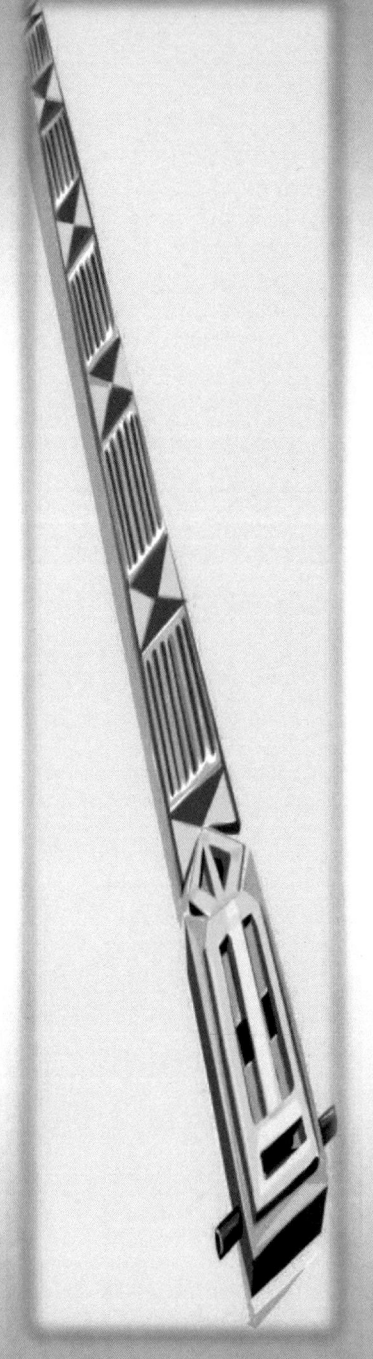

After many years together, Princess Kamala and Osei Tutu settled into a comfortable life. During these years, Princess Kamala gave birth to three children, two boys and one girl. The first boy, eight years, they named Prempeh II, (prim-pay), after King Prempeh I. The second boy, six years, was named Anokye (ar-no-chay), and the girl, three years, they named Yaa Asantewaa (yah-asante-wah). They called her YaYa for short. Over time, the couple's family duties increased, limiting their time to travel and collect the king's taxes once a month. Their trips away lasted at most one and a half weeks. During their leave, the children were in the care of Osei Tutu's aunt, Atieno (ar-tea-no).

Each time they travelled to collect the taxes, they were accompanied by eight to ten of the king's guards. Even though many years had passed since the war with King Timaeus in the east, Princess Kamala was still guarded. Everyone knew she still knew the secret to the location of the gold mines in the mountains. In addition, Osei Tutu was extremely important as the king's first nephew and one of his major advisors.

King Prempeh I summoned the two before him, after they returned home from a trip down country. He had received a message from the Dogon people in the north, requesting Princess Kamala travel to the Dogon region for an audience with the Dogan Oracle, their spiritual advisor.

King Prempeh I was very excited and honored by this request. The Dogan Oracle had the ability to heal and tell the future. There were always great benefits to any people from an audience with the oracle. But at the same time, he was concerned because he knew the trip would involve a great deal of time, energy, money, and many people. First, a caravan would have to be built. This caravan would need food and supplies, and have to pass through many regions with the permission from the chiefs of those regions to get to Dogon territory.

Above all, Princess Kamala would need a protective guard there and back. In addition, Osei Tutu said he would not let his wife travel that far by herself without him. These were some of the early considerations of King Prempeh I.

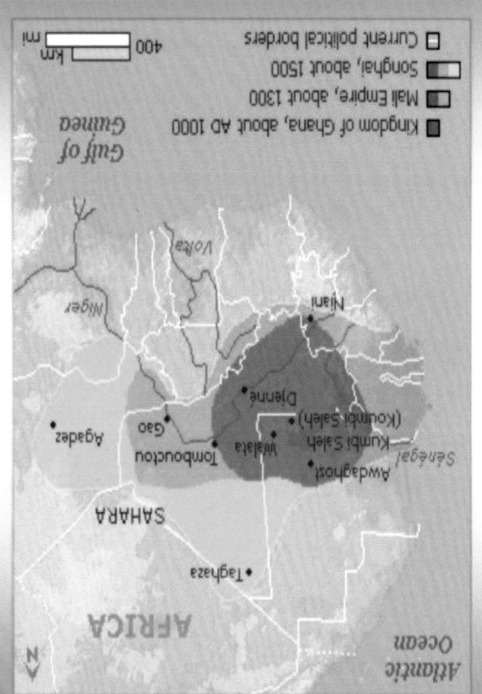

The Dogon people lived in a very dry, mountainous region of the country. Their oracle was very good at telling the future and had a deep understanding of cycles of weather based on the movement of the moon, stars, and planets.

The Dogon Oracle lived alone and had no contact with people. He never left his cave, so food and water had to be brought to him by selected servants in charge of his care. His isolation was the main focus of the tribe and considered extreme by outsiders. If it was found out that he had contact with people other than those in charge of his care, his life would be ended.

The Dogon Oracle was considered very sacred by all the people in the region, so this invitation generated a lot of talk throughout the entire western region.

King Prempeh I called a meeting of his advisors and councils of elders to discuss the logistics and financial obligations of the trip. Everyone knew that this expedition was going to be quite costly, so how to raise the money was the main topic of discussion.

All the advisors and elders agreed that the trip to the Dogon region would take place, so during the following weeks, the king and his advisors began to plan the journey. Food, water, camels, oxen, and shelters were gathered for the journey. Osei Tutu began purchasing camels, livestock, and oxen in open markets. King Prempeh I suggested they leave within the next two weeks, before the rainy season began.

Towards the end of the week, the caravan began to take shape in a line of oxen, wagons, king's guards, folded tents, baskets of food, water, gifts, and cloth.

To guarantee the safe passage of the caravan, King Prempeh I sent court messengers ahead to contact chiefs along the caravan's route. The chiefs in the villages along the routes must ensure the safety of all those in the caravan as it passes. Once their permission was given, they were presented with gifts from King Prempeh I.

Each time Princess Kamala and Osei Tutu travelled, they would leave their children in the care of Osei Tutu's aunt, Atieno. Those trips were short, not lasting more than two weeks. This trip to the Dogon territory, in the northern mountains, could last up to two months. The children would need provisions of food and clothing.

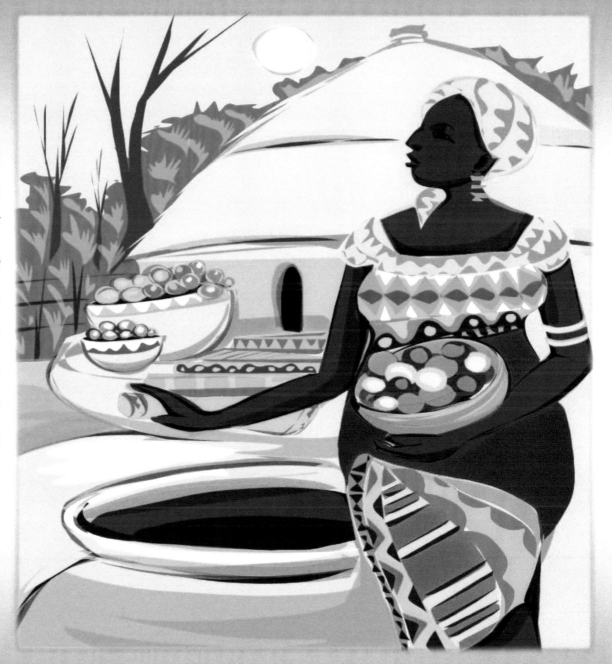

Princess Kamala was very upset that she would be away from her children for such a long time. Saying goodbye to her children was very emotional for the whole family.

Osei Tutu and Princess Kamala said goodbye to King Prempeh I, to the court, and to family and friends as they left the palace grounds to start their journey to the Dogon region.

The caravan left the court and travelled on the king's road for one week before they made their first stop at a village. The caravan camped there overnight and were offered food and water. Princess Kamala and Osei Tutu presented the chief with more gifts for the whole village.

After three weeks on the road, the caravan finally entered Dogon territory. They were met by twenty Dogon warriors and escorted to an area outside the village that had been cleared of brush and trees. The cleared area was alongside a stream that ran down the side of a mountain.

After they had set up camp and all the animals were watered and fed, a messenger from the chief appeared. "Welcome, I bring you greetings from my chief and our village. This evening, you and your wife are invited to dine with the chief and his family." Osei Tutu responded back, "We are happy to be in the land of the Dogon people and honored to accept the chief's invitation to dine with him this evening."

Osei Tutu and Princess Kamala at dinner with the Dogon chief and his family.

During dinner, the Dogon chief began to prepare the couple for the meeting with the Dogon Oracle. He explained to them the rules which governed the Dogon Oracle. "Let me begin by saying, it is most important that Princess Kamala not be on her menstrual cycle when the audience with the oracle takes place. Only Princess Kamala will be allowed to speak with the Dogon Oracle. Osei Tutu can not be present. He can walk with you to the base of the mountain, but will be prevented from going any further. Princess Kamala, you will be blindfolded and led through the mountains to the cave where the Dogon Oracle lives. Then, at the end of the audience with the oracle, you will be blindfolded again and led back down the mountain."

"The audience with the oracle will last for one hour and no more. At the end of the audience, you may ask the Dogon Oracle only three personal questions. The most important part of your audience will be to follow the instructions from the Dogon Oracle, no matter how absurd they seem to be. If you have any gifts for the oracle, you should give them to his caregivers. Under no circumstances are you to touch the oracle or make any physical contact with him. Do you have any questions?"

"Yes! When can I meet with the oracle?" Princess Kamala asked. "The oracle will send for you when he is ready," the Dogon chief replied.

The next five days, the group made themselves comfortable in their compound area. The village elders met with Osei Tutu to discuss affairs of state. Princess Kamala met with the village Queen Mothers to discuss some of the current female problems they were having.

In the evenings, they were entertained by local villages from the Dogon region. Each evening there were different dancers, musicians, singers, and story tellers to help them pass the time.

On their third evening, a Jeli (storyteller) entertained the group by telling the history of the Dogon people. He said, "In the beginning, the gods created man as a single birth possessing both male and female organs. The double-sexed hermaphrodite, we called a Jackal. This being was alone from birth, and there was disorder. It did horrible things on Earth that remain unspoken. The color given to this hermaphrodite was white, the same as death.

"The gods saw the confusion this being caused, so they instead created twins called Nummo/Nommo. Nummo were like serpents, green in color, more fish-like, and could change colors, at times having all the colors of the rainbow. The twins moved very slowly and stood upright on their tails. They were fish walking on land. They were called "Water Spirits," for they were both male and female. However, the Dogon considered them to be female since their symbol was the sun, so they were assigned the color red. The Nummo/Nommo saw that the original rule of twins was bound to disappear, and this original error might result in a being comparable to the Jackal, whose birth was single.

"It was because of the double-sexed hermaphrodite Jackal, born without a soul, that all humans after that had to be born single-sexed beings, to prevent a being like the Jackal from ever being born on Earth again."

The Jeli continued telling stories to the guests and villagers into the late evening.

The next day, six Dogon guards came into the compound and escorted Princess Kamala to meet with the Dogon Oracle.

Princess Kamala met the Dogon Oracle with his two caregivers present.

The Dogon Oracle began by telling her the story of the Dogon people but in more detail than the Jeli. "Have you heard the story of our creation from the village Jeli? His story of our creation is missing critical details.

"First, the Nummo/Nommo travelled to our planet because their star Sirius was dying. They were twins, and each one possessed both sexes (hermaphrodite). They had planned to live on Earth and combine their DNA with animals here to create a new life form they could inhabit.

"The experiment failed, and humans were the result. Not only was humanity created from this failure, but we became forever entwined to the alien Nummo/Nommo during sleep, in our dream time."

"I took this time to fill in the story of our creation, so you can better understand what I'm about to tell you. This information I will reveal to you today can only be shared with your King, Prempeh I. You cannot even tell your husband. He will press you to tell him, but you must not, under any circumstances.

"Princess Kamala, there is a famine coming to the whole western region. The famine will begin in the next two years with a loss of water to the region. The water loss will be very small at first, hardly noticed by the farmers. By the fifth year, it will be extreme. This loss of water will last for seven years, causing famine, war, animal migration, and death to the whole region. Your King Prempeh I can avoid this destruction by following the instructions I'm going to give you."

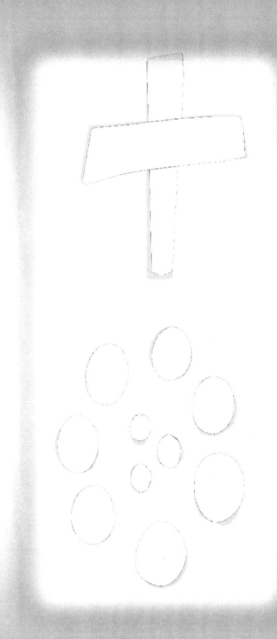

"It is most important for you to tell King Prempeh I to do seven things in the following order: One, bring all the chiefs and clan heads to meet at one time and tell them of this prophecy. Two, each region over the next seven years is to set aside one-fifth of their total crop in storage granaries. Three, each village must develop a patrol to watch over the granaries day and night. Four, any village with more than two thousand people should be divided into three sections and separated into smaller units. Five, a distribution center must be established in each section for the families to receive their food. Six, each village will elect an administrator who will organize the distribution and report monthly to King Prempeh I. Seven, start rationing food two years before the famine begins.

"If your king follows these instructions, the people will not suffer and his kingdom will stay strong. If he does not follow these instructions, there will be war, desolation, and death for his kingdom and the whole western region."

"You may now ask me your three questions, but first, I will tell you something personal. Your children are being abused by your sister-in-law. You cannot tell your husband or the king what she is doing."

Princess Kamala was shocked at this news and then asked the Dogon Oracle the following three questions: "How is she abusing them?" He said, "She is sending them out of the house for any mistake they make, no matter how small." "Why is she abusing them?" asked Princess Kamala. "She is jealous of your husband's relationship with King Prempeh I, and fears he will one day be king," the oracle replied. "How can I make her stop?" asked Princess Kamala. "You can't," replied the oracle.

The next day, the caravan left the Dogon village and headed back home.

During their first evening on the road back home, Osei Tutu became curious about the meeting between his wife and the Dogon Oracle. At dinner, he questioned Princess Kamala on what the Dogon Oracle told her. So that her husband would not feel excluded, she told him that the oracle gave her information about crop growth and special plants to be used for healing.

She then asked her husband, "Can we stop in Djenne` to visit Mom and Dad on our way back home?" He agreed and said, "Yes! It would be a nice break from the road, and I could use a good home-cooked meal."

When Princess Kamala arrived at her family's village, everyone came out to greet and welcome them. General Zunni and his warriors were standing guard as they entered the gates.

The village was so happy to see Princess Kamala and Osei Tutu that they planned a big feast in their honor. During the feast, Princess Kamala took a moment to speak alone with Kimathi, her long-time friend and confident. "King Prempeh I will request that a representative from every village in the region be sent to the palace. Kimathi, it's very important that you be chosen to represent our village. But most critical is that you stay at court for a period of time to observe what happens to my children when Osei Tutu and I travel to do tax collection for the king. My audience with the Dogon Oracle revealed that Atieno, Osei Tutu's aunt, is abusing my children when Osei Tutu and I travel away. I can't tell Osei Tutu of the abuse because it would cause a family split that could possibly bring down Prempeh I's reign.

"After all these years at court, I'm still an outsider and not of royal blood. Kimathi, I need you to be my eyes and tell me what is going on at Atieno's house with my children. Just watch, but don't attempt to interfere. I don't know how to solve this problem yet, but the more information I can get about what Atieno is actually doing to the children will help me initiate any action. Kimathi, please be very discreet because this is the court of Prempeh I and Atieno and the children are blood royals of that court."

Kimathi and Princess Kamala talked privately during the feast held in her honor.

The Caravan arrives back home at the king's palace.

As soon as they returned home, Princess Kamala was summoned to an audience with the king. She told King Prempeh I, in detail, exactly what the Dogon Oracle said and his specific instructions to hold the region together.

Then the King said in a very serious voice, "Now Princess Kamala, I have only one question. Have you told this information to anyone other than me on your journey home?" "Absolutely, not," Princess Kamala replied. "I told no one this information but you. Not even my husband knows."

Over the next four months, King Prempeh I started the plan advised by the Dogon Oracle. He called together advisors, elders, and clan heads from all over the western region and in other areas that would be affected by the famine. Each group met with the king and then decided amongst themselves how to work out details of the plan the Dogon Oracle suggested. All the villages in the region elected a liaison to report their monthly progress to the king's administrator. The plan included certain crops to be grown, special structures to be built to house and store the provisions, water wells to be dug, areas to be cleared for new smaller village sites, and the population to be prepared for the famine that was to come.

Kimathi became the liaison representative for his village and travelled back and forth from his village to the court. Princess Kamala provided him with a temporary residence at court not far from her and Osei Tutu's compound. When Osei Tutu and she had to travel to other villages to collect the king's taxes, Kimathi made arrangements to be at court as an unannounced observer of Atieno's care of Princess Kamala's children.

On an evening in late summer, when both parents were gone, Kimathi heard yelling and screaming as he walked past Atieno's compound. Not wanting to appear nosy, he walked around to the back of her compound to see what was happening inside. Suddenly, in the dark, he saw three children running from the house into the forest. Chasing close behind was Atieno, yelling and screaming with a large stick in her hand.

Kimathi followed the children into the forest. He watched them as they made themselves comfortable in a cave. He could hear sounds coming from the cave but he did not go in.

The children spent the entire night in the cave and did not reappear in the village until sunrise the next morning. He could see them inside Atieno's compound eating porridge with her children.   Later in the afternoon, Kimathi was able to get the children alone and questioned them on their escape to the forest.

Prempeh II said, "Aunt Atieno often got angry with us and would chase us out of the house or beat us with her stick." "She beat the other children too, but never chased them from the house into the forest," Anoke said. Kimathi asked, "So why did you stay all night in the forest cave?" "We felt safe in the cave with our friends. Besides, Aunt Atieno would not let us back in the house once we left," Yaya replied.

When Osei Tutu and Princess Kamala returned home, Kimathi told Princess Kamala what he had observed. "From my observation, the children spent the night in the forest huddled together with their friends." Princess Kamala asked, "Who are their forest friends?" Kimathi said, "They would not tell me."

Princess Kamala realized she had a serious problem to solve. If she told her husband about the abuse, he would tell his uncle, King Prempeh I, who would demand an explanation from Atieno. Osei Tutu, the son of King Prempeh I's youngest brother, would argue with Atieno, the king's eldest sister. Atieno was in the direct blood line to establish the next successor to King Prempeh I. She was very powerful at court and very envious of the close relationship between Osei Tutu and the king, because the king spent many hours in council with Osei Tutu and no time with her son. Atieno often voiced her feelings in court that Osei Tutu might try to usurp the throne from her side of the family. Even though Princess Kamala and Osei Tutu had been happily married for ten years, Atieno never liked Princess Kamala or accepted her as Osei Tutu's wife because she was not of royal blood or a wealthy family. This fact gave Atieno's words even more power in the family's eyes.

During open court ceremonies, Atieno would always suggest that Osei Tutu take a second wife from a wealthy family in the north. Osei Tutu ignored her remarks and always assured Princess Kamala that she was the only woman for him. Princess Kamala considered all these things as she thought about a solution to her problem. She could not leave her children with Atieno again after what Kimathi had told her, so she pretended to be sick when it was time for her and Osei Tutu to travel. After a while, the king demanded that they both travel to the northern region to collect taxes.

Princess Kamala did not know how long she and Osei Tutu would be gone, so she prepared the children to survive in her absence. She collected extra food, water, clothing, and tools. She then hid them in the forest and showed the children where they were. She gave them as many tools as she thought they would need to survive while she was away.

The children living in the forest near a cave, playing with three baby leopard cubs.

Princess Kamala and Osei Tutu returned home to find the children in their compound well cared for and eating porridge for breakfast. There was a fire going with a large pot of water heating up for food and washing.

With the greatest amount of excitement, Yaya explained, "Mama, Aunt Atieno is sick and can't get out of bed, so King Prempeh I sent his house servants to care for us."

Atieno was weak and confined to her bed. The family gathered around her sick bed to pray for her to recover.

The healers of three villages came to cure Atieno. They worked over her for four days, but could not cure her ailment. Each day, the rash on her body spread, and she became weaker. Everyone at court knew of the rash that covered her arms and was spreading to other areas of her body. They did not know if it was contagious, so they kept their distance and stayed away from her compound. As time passed, her major caregivers were Princess Kamala and her own house servants.

One evening after Princess Kamala returned from a visit to Atieno, her middle son, Anokye, spoke to her about something he saw the monkeys in the forest do to each other. "Mama, we saw that when the monkeys had a rash on their skin, they used a special leaf from a tree to get rid of it. They chewed the leaf up, spit it back out, then rubbed it into the open sores on their skin. In a few days, the rash was gone without a trace, and they would be back to playing with each other in the trees." Princess Kamala asked, "Anokye, can you find the leaf and bring it to me, so I can make a poultice for Atieno?"

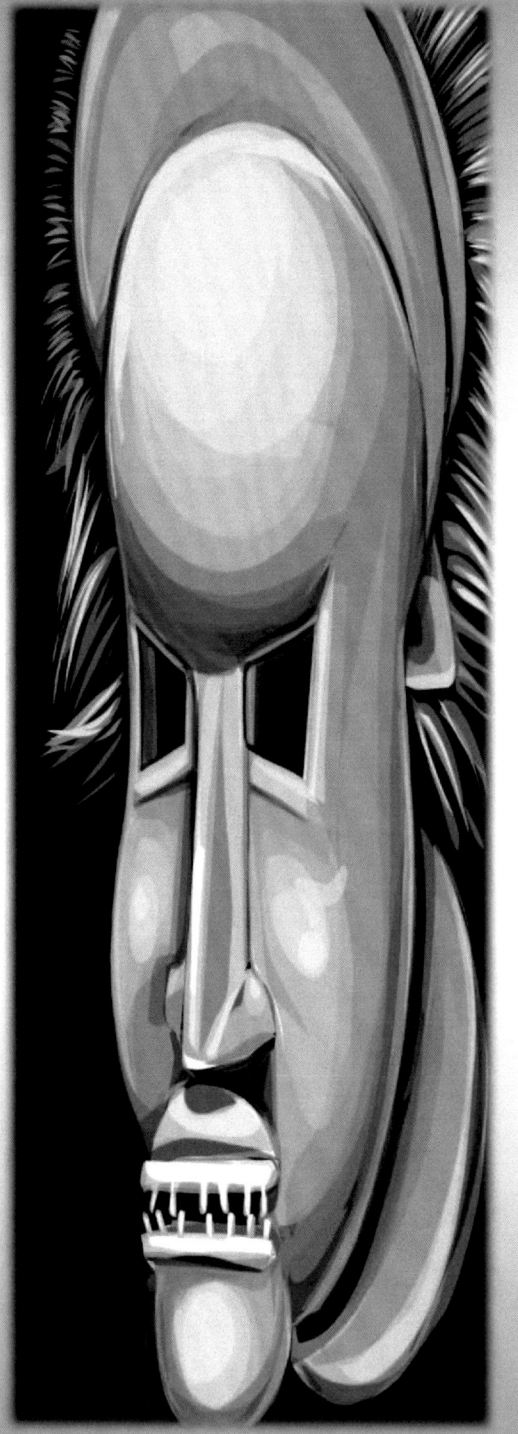

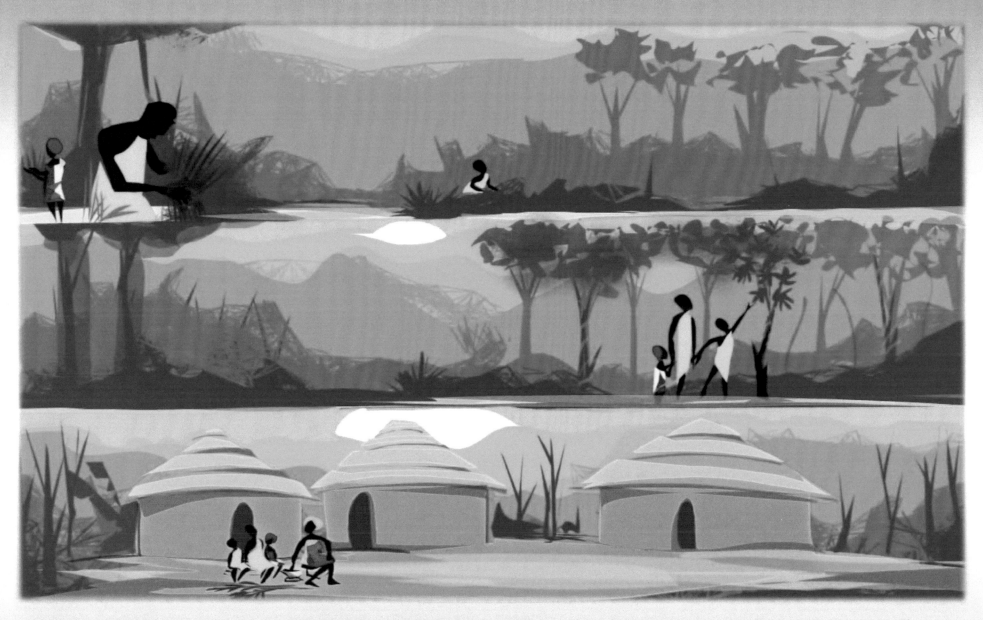

That afternoon, the three children went into the forest to look for the leaves that might heal Atieno's rash.

42

Just before dark, the children found the leaves and brought them to their mother. Princess Kamala made a poultice and treated Atieno with it. By the end of the week, Atieno was out of bed, eating, and on her way to a full recovery.

After Atieno recovered, she visited Princess Kamala's compound to thank her for what she had done to save her life. Princess Kamala explained how her children found the remedy. "When you forced my children to sleep in the forest overnight, they observed the monkeys rubbing each other with the special leaves. So I sent them into the forest to find these leaves. They spent the whole day in the forest until they found them, Atieno." Atieno replied, "I am so very ashamed of how I treated your children. Please, Princess Kamala, forgive me. I was afraid you and Osei Tutu would take the throne from my son." "I forgive you Atieno, but you must promise to never mistreat my children again whenever they are left in your care." "I promise, but please don't tell the king or Osei Tutu." "Don't worry, I won't."

When King Prempeh I heard how Princess Kamala's children saved Atieno's life, he honored each of them at court with their own Kente cloth pattern and a hectare of land. All the family members were present, and Aunt Atieno stood proudly behind the children as they were honored.

As King Prempeh I continued with the plans to offset the famine, his administrator reported to him that some of the villages in the eastern region had refused to participate. They didn't believe that the famine was real or would impact their area. The administrator suggested that the king make a state visit to the region to reinforce his provisions and laws. The administrator suggested that it would serve the realm even better if the king visited all five regions and met with the chiefs and elders of those areas to bring them up to date on the progress throughout the entire realm. King Prempeh I agreed and suggested the best time of year to do this would be after the rainy season.

After the rainy season was over, the king met with each of his chiefs and elders in all the regions. Just about all of them said that it was a good idea to save some of their crops each season, but they could not afford to build the structures to house the excess crops as well as pay their regular taxes that were assessed to their villages. King Prempeh I understood the problem, so he made a decision to suspend all taxes during this time of preparation for the coming famine.

Special structures, built off the ground where food was to be stored, dotted the landscape and the horizon.

The years passed slowly, and when the famine came, King Prempeh I's region had more than enough food. There was such an abundance of food that the administrator arranged to sell food to other regions where the people were starving because they had not prepared for the famine.

King Prempeh I was so grateful to the Dogon Oracle and pleased with how everything had turned out that he sent an emissary to the Dogon people with food and gifts for all those who aided.

King Prempeh I honored Princess Kamala with five chests of gold and five hectares of land for bringing the Dogon message to him and following the oracle's instructions.

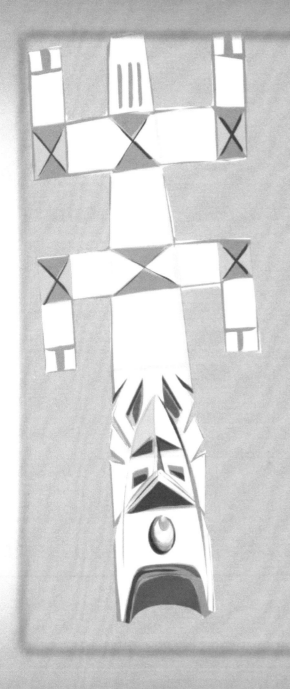

Conclusion

Princess Kamala was presented with a very difficult dilemma. If she had told her husband about the abuse to her children, Atieno would have been called before the king and denied all the accusations. Because Princess Kamala was not of royal blood, she would not likely be believed. Once doubt was cast on her word, King Prempeh I would have been less likely to believe in her message from the Dogon Oracle. Lack of credibility in her word would have resulted in a major upheaval for the region and the future reign of King Prempeh I. Her only solution was to protect her children by giving them the tools and supplies that would enable them to survive.

To the reader: Each new day our families are often confronted with problems that appear to have no solutions. The job of daily living is to solve these problems in an orderly manner. By concentrating and thinking through the possible solutions and their effects, we can put our lives in order.

Footnote 1

Matrilineal cultures trace identity through the mother's line of descent. Within this system, a person of either sex inherits property and titles passed down from his or her mother. The traditional Asante of Ghana base their economic, political, and social organizations on matrilineal descent from a particular ancestral mother. Each lineage controls their land, supervises marriages of its members, and settles internal disputes within its membership. The result of this system is a man's nephew (sister's son) will have priority over the man's own son.

Footnote 2

Research shows that the Dogon religion is the world's original mythology. It began in Africa long before humans migrated to other areas of the planet. Fragments of the Dogon religion exist as part of most religions all over the world. Dogon mythology involves amphibious beings from a dying planet visiting earth and combining their DNA to produce human beings. They called the dying planet Sirius. According to the Dogon, it was Nummo who taught them about the stars, planets, and knowledge of DNA. Most of this information is intertwined into Dogon daily life. In this way they can recall it and pass it down to the next generation.

Bibliography

Wittle, Marleen (2001), Long Live the Dead: Changing funeral celebration in Asante, Ghana. Pg55

Bedaux, R.& J.D. Van der Waals (eds.) (2003) Dogon: Myth & Reality in Mali. Leiden: Museum of Ethnology.